pointing

stretching

tickling

finding

hiding

climbing

standing

marching

waiting

For Alice

This book belongs to:

KIRSTEN MORAG.

First published 1994 by Walker Books Ltd
87 Vauxhall Walk, London SE11 5HJ

2 4 6 8 10 9 7 5 3 1

This book has been typeset in Plantin Light.

Printed in Italy

British Library Cataloguing in Publication Data
A catalogue record for this book is available from the British Library.

ISBN 0-7445-3249-3

Hiding

Shirley Hughes

WALKER BOOKS
LONDON

You can't see me, I'm hiding!

Here I am.

I'm hiding again!

Bet you can't find me this time!

Under a bush in the garden
is a very good place to hide.

So is a big
umbrella,

or down at the end
of the bed.

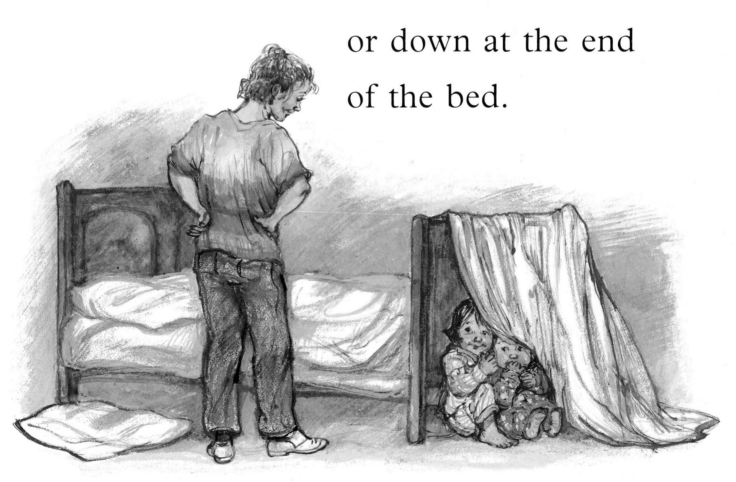

Sometimes Dad hides
behind a newspaper.

And Mum hides behind a
book on the sofa.

You can even hide under a hat.

Tortoises hide inside their shells
when they aren't feeling friendly,

and hamsters hide right at the
back of their cages when they
want to go to sleep.

When the baby hides his eyes
he thinks you can't see him.
But he's there all the time!

A lot of things seem to hide –
the moon behind the clouds,

and the sun behind the trees.

Flowers need to hide in the ground
in wintertime.

But they come peeping out again
in the spring.

Buster always hides when it's time

for his bath,

and so does Mum's purse when we're
all ready to go out shopping.

Our favourite place to hide is behind the
kitchen door. Then we jump out – BOO!

And can you guess who's hiding behind these curtains?

You're right!
Now we're coming out –
is everyone clapping?

pulling

balancing

measuring

teaching

hiding

sliding

cooking

tasting

throwing